This breakfast belongs to:

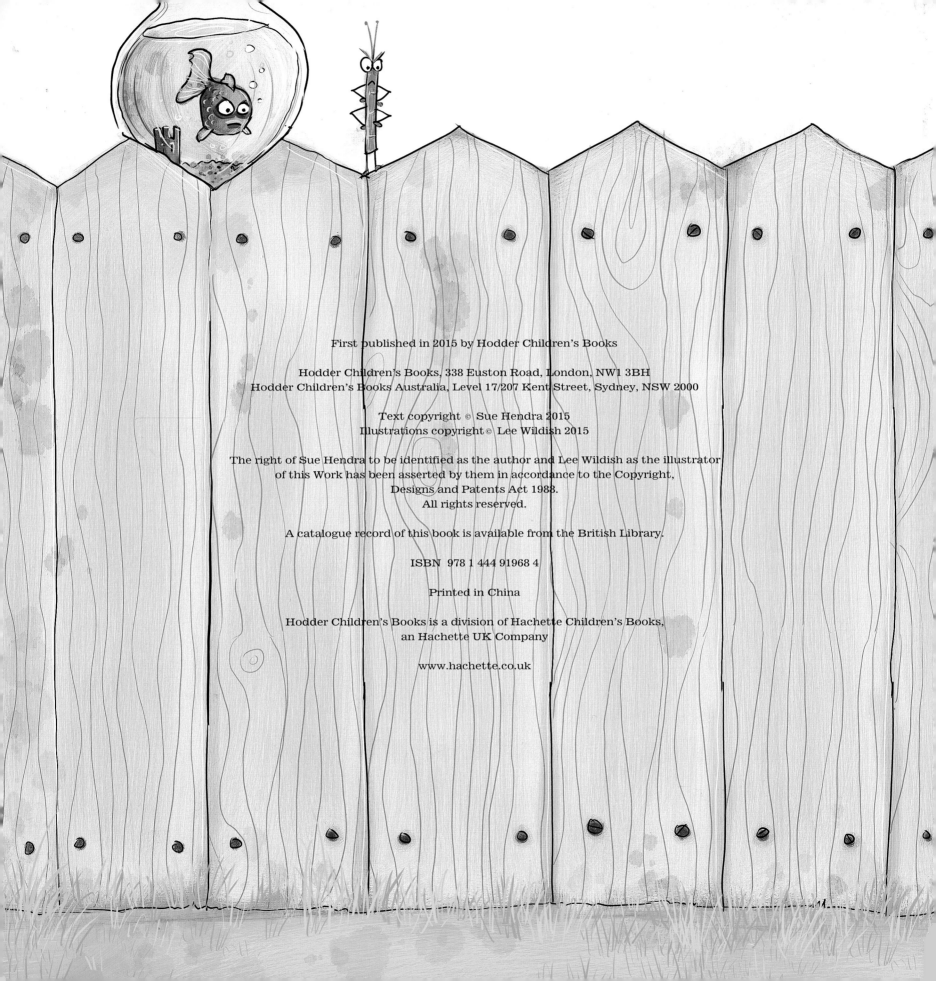

First published in 2015 by Hodder Children's Books

Hodder Children's Books, 338 Euston Road, London, NW1 3BH
Hodder Children's Books Australia, Level 17/207 Kent Street, Sydney, NSW 2000

A catalogue record of this book is available from the British Library.

ISBN 978 1 444 91968 4

Printed in China

Hodder Children's Books is a division of Hachette Children's Books,
an Hachette UK Company

www.hachette.co.uk

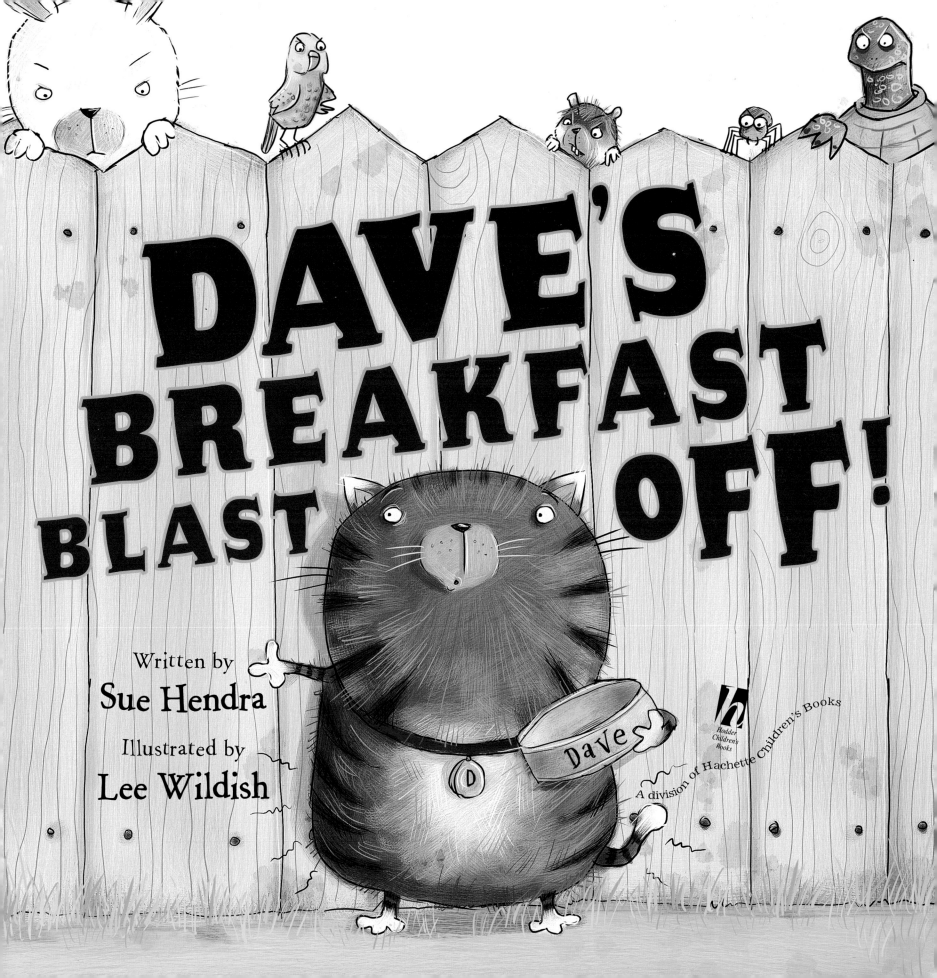

DAVE'S BREAKFAST BLAST OFF!

Written by
Sue Hendra

Illustrated by
Lee Wildish

Hodder Children's Books

A division of Hachette Children's Books

Dave was big and quite fantastic, and so were his breakfasts.

After a long snooze and a big stretch,
he trotted into the kitchen.
But Dave was in
for a shock...

His bowl was
EMPTY!
EMPTY!
EMPTY!
EMPTY!
EMPTY!

Dave waited...

and waited...

and waited...

and waited.

But the bowl was still empty!
Luckily Bug had an idea.

'Let's go out for breakfast!'

Dave stuck his head out of the cat flap.
His rumbling tummy got everyone's
attention. Bug explained the plan.

Hedgehog
stood on Squirrel,
Bird stood on Hedgehog
(ouch!), Mouse stood on
Bird, and together they
hoofed Dave over the fence
to look for breakfast next door.

Sure enough, there was a breakfast!
It was a little breakfast, but it was
still a breakfast. Surely Budgie wouldn't
mind if Dave had a tiny taste…

HMMM,
crunchy, thought Dave.

RUMBLE, RUMBLE. He was still hungry.
Surely Hamster wouldn't
mind if Dave had a little nibble...

HMMM, crispy, thought Dave.

RUMBLE, RUMBLE.

He was still hungry,
but Rabbit's carrots
would never fill Dave up.

He ate fish food,

spider food,

stick insect food,

tortoise food,

and smelly socks.
Hang on a minute,
that isn't even food!

But Dave was still hungry.

Suddenly Dave's tummy made a different noise...

...pING, BOING, FLOLLOP, FU-DU-DU-DU-D, and another FLOLLOP.

But just then Dave saw something amazing...

Now *that's* breakfast!
Maybe he could just have a little bite...

But Dog
wasn't happy.

The other pets weren't happy.
Dave's tummy wasn't happy either...
He had eaten too many breakfasts!
Dog came closer...

Dave's tummy was out of control, but there was nothing he could do to stop it.

...PING, BOING, FU-DU-DU-DU-D, FLOLLOP

5 4 3 2 1...

went Dave's tummy. Something big was about to happen.

It had been a long, hard morning for Dave.
But not to worry, it was almost
LUNCHTIME!